A CHINESE FOLKTALE
THE
CRICKET'S CAGE

RETOLD BY STEFAN CZERNECKI

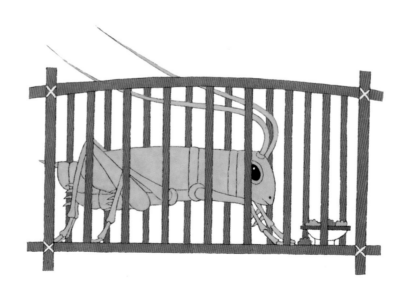

HYPERION BOOKS FOR CHILDREN
NEW YORK

Hundreds of years ago in China, there lived an emperor of the Ming dynasty named Yongle (Yung-lo). His love of architecture drove him to create an imperial palace the likes of which had never before been seen. Surrounded by a great wall, the complex was called the Forbidden City. To make the structure even more grand, Yongle ordered that plans be drawn to create four towers—one on each corner of the wall.

Soon after, Wu Zhong (Woo Chung), his most trusted minister, spread before Yongle some sheets of mulberry paper outlining intricate designs for the towers.

"Do you call these plans?" the emperor demanded. "Where is the grace, the beauty? I want my towers to be magnificent. Is there no one in this land who can design a structure of suitable elegance? Take these scratchings away."

Wu Zhong bowed deeply and removed the offending papers. The day before he had presented a different set of plans, but the emperor's reaction was the same. Nothing pleased him. Master Builder Cai Xin (Ts-eye Sin) had drawn sixteen different designs over the past six weeks but they were all deemed too plain or too high or too ugly.

Two months went by and still Yongle rejected every design Cai Xin produced. The emperor was growing impatient. He summoned Wu Zhong and said, "These towers must be so impressive that anyone who sees them will be reminded of the power and splendor of my kingdom. I am tired of waiting. If you do not present a suitable idea within three days you will lose your head."

"What can I do?" Wu Zhong wailed when he was outside the palace. Angrily he kicked the stones along the path. Then he summoned Cai Xin and told him, "If a plan that pleases the emperor is not forthcoming in two days I will see that you lose your head."

Cai Xin knew that the minister had great power and feared for his life. That afternoon he went to the house of the carpenter Kuai Xiang (Kw-eye See-ang) and said, "You are a lazy dog. Your models are no good. Why can't you build something spectacular? If I do not have a proper model within one day I will see that you lose your head."

Kuai Xiang stared at the little sticks of millet on his worktable but could not think of a way to arrange them. He wasn't trained to build without a plan. In despair he left his house and walked aimlessly down the road. When he came to the local marketplace he stopped to tell his story to a friend who sold crickets.

"You are in great trouble," his friend agreed. "Please allow me to give you my best singer. His song will surely bring you good luck and cheer you up as well."

When Kuai Xiang got home with his new pet he set the tiny cage at the corner of his worktable. The cricket rubbed his front wing covers together and made beautiful music.

"You do cheer me up," Kuai Xiang said as he dipped his brush into his ink box and tried to create a design that he could build. After several attempts he could not think of a tower to draw and decided that his efforts were useless. Walking to the wall he lifted down the pipa (pee-pah) and began to play softly to accompany the cricket's song.

"Dear little cricket," Kuai Xiang said, "I will call you Pipa because your music reminds me of this wonderful instrument." Later the carpenter put soft fruit and lettuce in tiny dishes and then prepared for bed. "I do not have long to live," he said, "but I will build you a larger cage and leave you in comfort before I go."

知了歌

知了，知了，

一樣樣是命，

不一定就蟲低人高

知了，知了，

一樣樣是朋友，

解難時不分他是人還是小咬．

知了，知了，

一樣樣是囚徒，

住在皇宮未必就勝過蟲巢．

知了，知了，

萬般由人變化，

一切還是天地創造．

Pipa tried to sleep but his stubby body ached and his legs were cramped. I hope my new cage has many levels so I have more space, and many pillars and crossbars so I can crawl about more freely, he thought. I'm sure my master would do everything in his power to please me if I could only tell him what I want. As the cricket tried to turn around he bumped against the cage door causing it to open. Cautiously he crawled out.

When his antennae touched the carved ink box he had an idea. He dipped his long antennae into the gooey black depths and coated them well. He then hurried over to a large piece of mulberry paper fastened at the corner of the table.

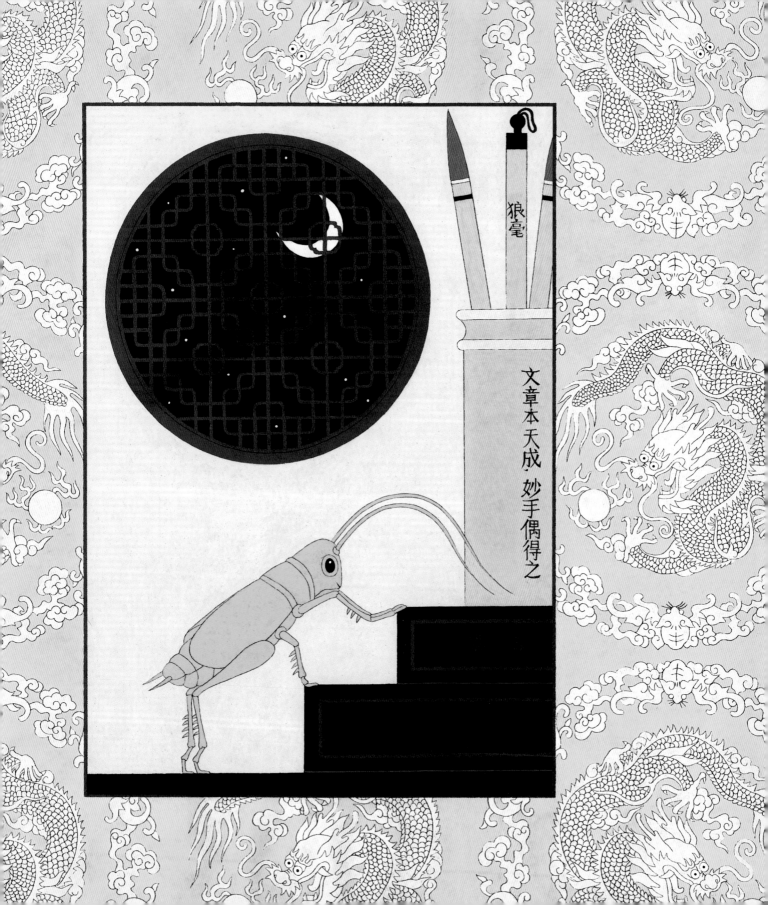

Slowly Pipa began making black marks on the smooth surface as he had seen Kuai Xiang do. When his antennae were dry he made his way back to the ink box and returned to draw more lines and characters. All night he traveled back and forth until the paper was covered with a plan for a cricket cage. It had nine beams, eighteen pillars, and seventy-two roof ridges—a spectacular miniature pavilion more elegant than any cage he had ever seen. Exhausted, the cricket crawled back into his tiny home and went to sleep.

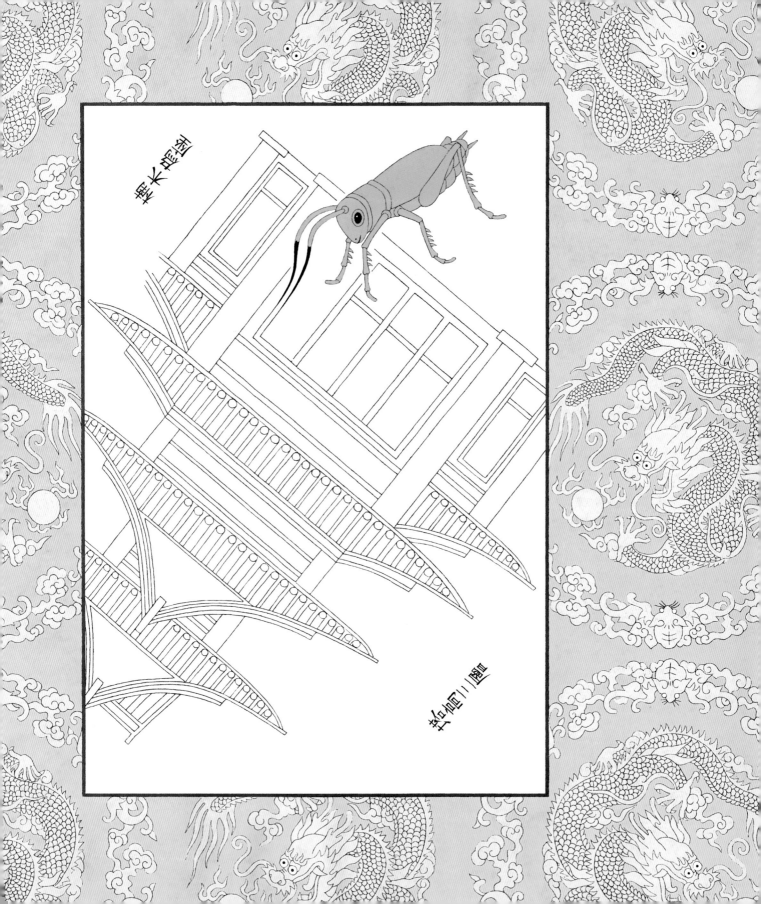

In the morning when Kuai Xiang approached his worktable he noticed the paper covered with black ink. Where did this come from? he wondered. The plans were so splendid and every detail so precise that he forgot his troubles and immediately set to work on Pipa's cage. While Kuai Xiang worked the cricket sang his wonderful songs. At last the towering miniature was finished. "There," he said. "A perfect home for my cricket."

Late in the afternoon Cai Xin arrived to see what progress had been made on the model for the emperor's towers.

"I'm afraid I have been unable to fulfill your command," Kuai Xiang said dejectedly.

"What are you talking about?" cried Cai Xin. "This is perfect! You have made the most beautiful and unusual tower model I have ever seen. Let us find Wu Zhong immediately. Ah, what a fortunate day."

Kuai Xiang was confused. He began to explain that it was only a cricket cage but Cai Xin would hear nothing of it. Kuai Xiang placed the cricket back in his old cage and the two men set off for the palace. "I hope to make you another cage this evening, dear Pipa," Kuai Xiang called softly as he went out the door.

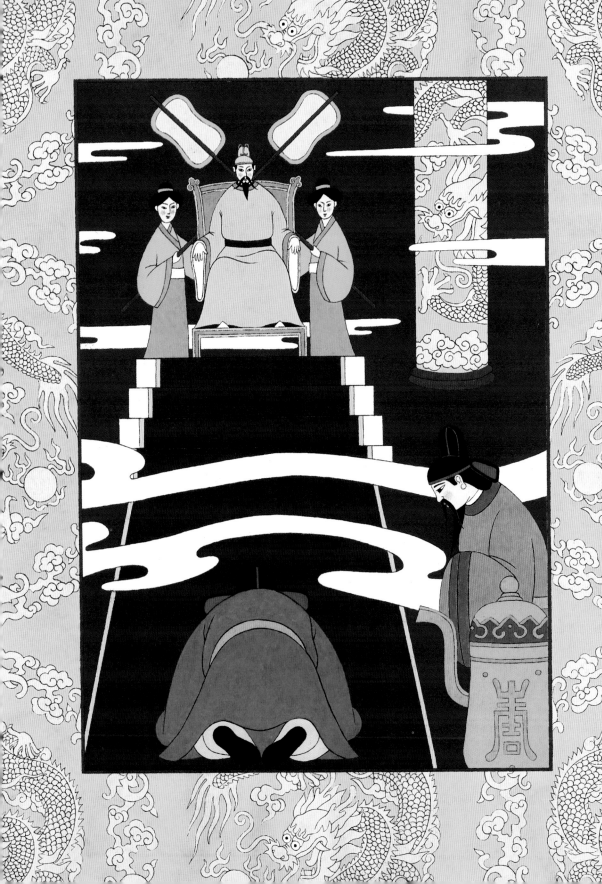

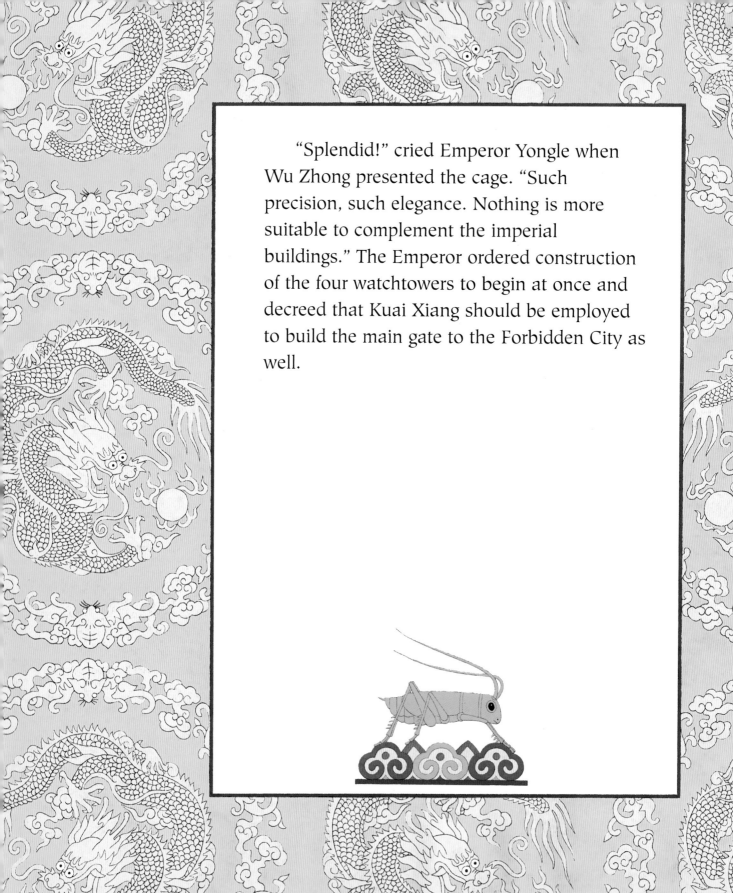

"Splendid!" cried Emperor Yongle when Wu Zhong presented the cage. "Such precision, such elegance. Nothing is more suitable to complement the imperial buildings." The Emperor ordered construction of the four watchtowers to begin at once and decreed that Kuai Xiang should be employed to build the main gate to the Forbidden City as well.

"I owe it all to you, dear cricket," Kuai Xiang told his pet that evening. "You have brought me good fortune." Thereafter the tiny cricket went everywhere with Kuai Xiang. Over time he had many different cages but none as fine as the one that became the model for the royal watchtowers.

For my friend Gu Xiong

Author's Note

Hundreds of years ago in China, the third emperor of the Ming dynasty, Yongle, decided to move the country's capital north from Nanjing to the old Mongol city of Kanbalu (later called Dadu), where he had been stationed as a young prince. Zhu Yuanzhang, founding emperor of the Ming dynasty, called it Peiping, which Yongle later renamed Beijing, meaning "northern capital." His father, the first emperor, had driven out the Mongol invaders from China, and Yongle was anxious to keep the country strong and united. First he completed the Great Wall across northern China that had been started years before. His armies used it to guard against enemy attack. Then he restored the imperial palace which he wanted to be the crowning glory of all his accomplishments.

The royal buildings of Kanbalu built by the Mongols were in disrepair. Yongle renovated them and contained them within a thick red brick wall, three-quarters of a mile square. This enclosure was called the Forbidden City. To present an even grander appearance from the outside, Emperor Yongle decided to add a magnificent watchtower at each corner of the wall. The legend of how they were built is related in *The Cricket's Cage*.

This Chinese folktale has been told by generations of Beijing storytellers. It is collected in a book called *Beijing Legends* (Beijing Publishing House, 1957), which was compiled by Jin Shoushen (1906–68), a Manchu scholar. The tale in the book is called "The Cricket Cage Peddler" and was translated by Cimon Ching for Stefan Czernecki.

In China, people keep crickets as pets for the music they produce. Only male crickets "sing," by rubbing their front wing covers together. Their songs are believed to bring good fortune. Though children may keep their crickets in clay jars, the pets are often housed in elaborate cages. Built from millet (grain stalks), bamboo, and even gold, the cages sometimes contain tiny dishes and furniture and usually travel about with their owners. The crickets are encouraged to sing by a tickler made of rat whiskers fastened to a reed.

The pipa is a four-stringed instrument more than two thousand years old. It makes a sweet, chirping sound.

Printed in Hong Kong.

FIRST EDITION
10 9 8 7 6 5 4 3 2 1

Library of Congress Cataloging-in-Publication Data
Czernecki, Stefan.
        The cricket's cage : a Chinese folktale / retold and illustrated by Stefan Czernecki :
[translated by Cimon Ching]. — 1st ed.
            p.   cm.
        Includes a poem translated by Amugulang Honiqin.
        Summary: Retells a Chinese folktale in which a clever and kindly cricket is
responsible for designing the tower buildings for Beijing's "Forbidden City."
        ISBN 0-7868-0296-0 (trade)—ISBN 0-7868-2234-1 (lib. bdg.)
        [1. Crickets—Folklore. 2. Folklore—China.] I. Ching, Cimon. II. Title.
PZ8.1.C994Cr 1997
398.2'095104525726—dc20   96-15407
[E]

Translation of Chinese poem, *I See Song*,
by Amugulang Honiqin on page 17

I see, I see. Life is the same.
Humans are not necessarily higher
  than bugs.
I see, I see. Friends are the same.
No matter if it's a man or a bug.
I see, I see. Prisoners are the same.
Although some may dwell in palaces.
I see, I see that heaven and earth
  create everything.
It is humans that change things.

The artwork was prepared using Chinese mineral and vegetable pigments. The embroidered design of the borders represents the emperor's robes, and during Yongle's dynasty only he could wear the color yellow. This book is set in 14-point Hiroshige Book.